There are four thousand different kinds of crickets.
Some live underground, others above.
Some live in shrubs or trees, and some even live in water.
Both male and female crickets can hear,
but only the male can make a sound.
By rubbing his wings together he chirps.
Some people say that it sounds like a song!

For Sally and Bob

Eric Carle  The Very Quiet Cricket

Scholastic Book Club Edition

One warm day,
from a tiny egg
a little cricket was born.

Welcome! chirped a big cricket,
rubbing his wings together.
The little cricket wanted to answer,
so he rubbed his wings together.
But nothing happened. Not a sound.

Good morning! whizzed a locust,
spinning through the air.
The little cricket wanted to answer,
so he rubbed his wings together.
But nothing happened. Not a sound.

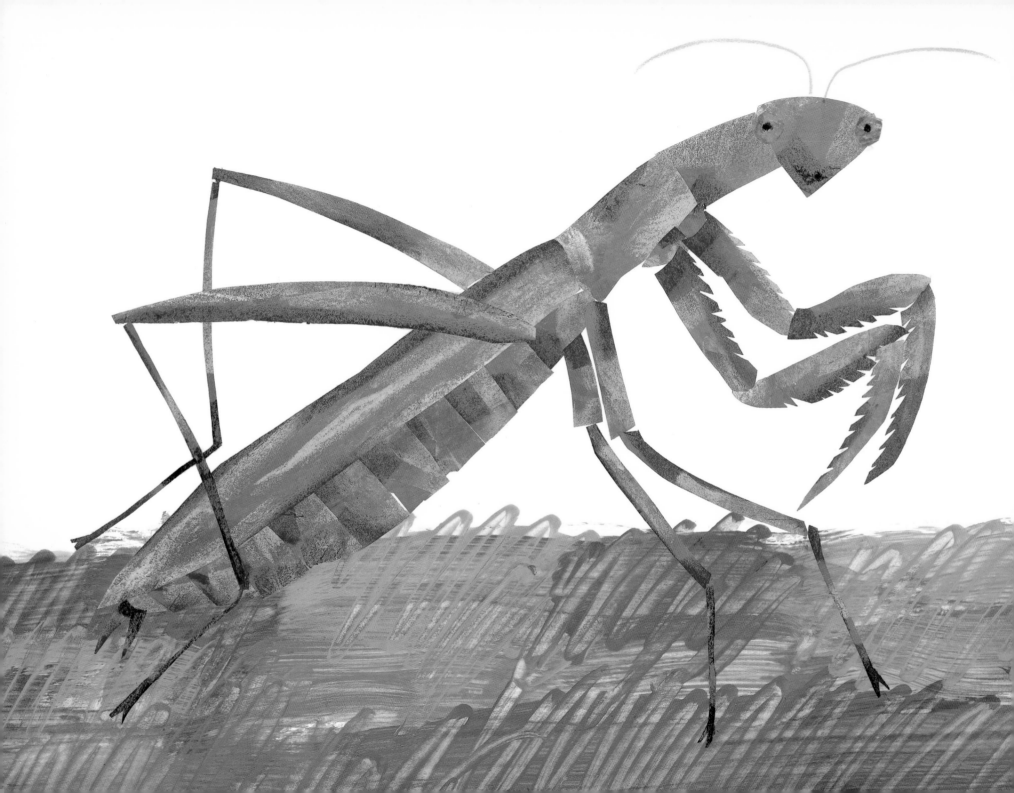

Hello! whispered a praying mantis,
scraping its huge front legs together.
The little cricket wanted to answer,
so he rubbed his wings together.
But nothing happened. Not a sound.

Good day! crunched a worm,
munching its way out of an apple.
The little cricket wanted to answer,
so he rubbed his wings together.
But nothing happened. Not a sound.

Hi! bubbled a spittlebug,
slurping in a sea of froth.
The little cricket wanted to answer,
so he rubbed his wings together.
But nothing happened. Not a sound.

Good afternoon! screeched a cicada,
clinging to a branch of a tree.
The little cricket wanted to answer,
so he rubbed his wings together.
But nothing happened. Not a sound.

How are you! hummed a bumblebee,
flying from flower to flower.
The little cricket wanted to answer,
so he rubbed his wings together.
But nothing happened. Not a sound.

Good evening! whirred a dragonfly,
gliding above the water.
The little cricket wanted to answer,
so he rubbed his wings together.
But nothing happened. Not a sound.

Good night! buzzed the mosquitoes,
dancing among the stars.
The little cricket wanted to answer,
so he rubbed his wings together.
But nothing happened. Not a sound.

A luna moth sailed
quietly through the night.
And the cricket
enjoyed the stillness.

As the luna moth disappeared
silently into the distance,
the cricket saw another cricket.
She, too, was a very quiet cricket.

Then he rubbed his wings together
one more time.
And this time...

...he chirped the most beautiful sound that she had ever heard.

I hope you have enjoyed this story.
Close the book now and your cricket's
chirp will have a long life.

Eric Carle

ISBN 0-590-46452-3

Copyright © 1990 by Eric Carle Corp.
All rights reserved. Published by Scholastic Inc.,
730 Broadway, New York, NY 10003, by arrangement with
Philomel Books, a division of The Putnam & Grosset Book Group.

12 11 10 9 8 7 6 5 4 3 2 1   3 4 5 6 7 8/9

Printed in China

First Scholastic printing, January 1993